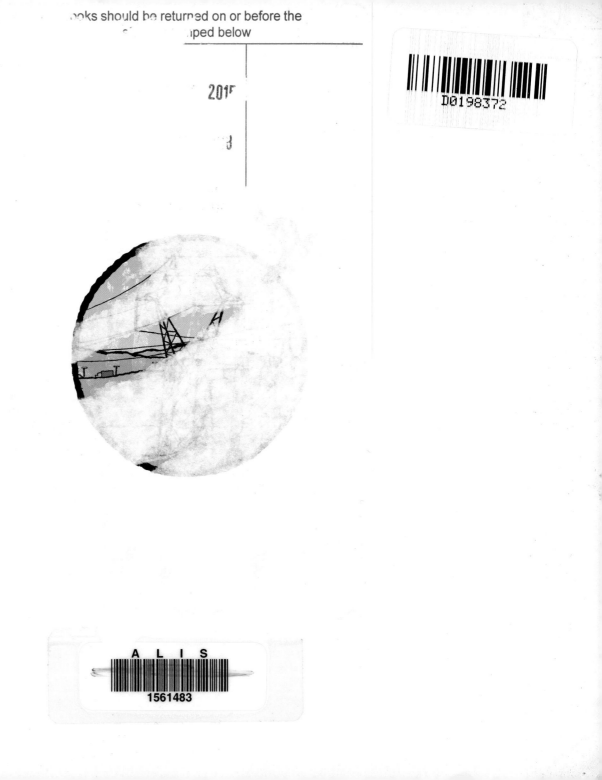

Always stay well away from pylons and electric power lines. The electricity that travels through them is so strong it could kill you!

SCIENCE WORKS

CHARGING ABOUT

THE STORY OF ELECTRICITY

THIS WILL BRIGHTEN UP MY DAY.

Jacqui Bailey • Matthew Lilly

A & C BLACK • LONDON

It was a bright sunny morning, but the weather forecast said there was a storm on the way.

Thick grey clouds rolled into view and by midday there wasn't a patch of blue to be seen.

The sky grew dark and gloomy.

In the town, lights went on in shops and offices, and drivers flicked on their headlights.

IT LOOKS LIKE HEAVY RAIN, WITH SOME THUNDER AND LIGHTNING AHEAD...

People switched on lights at home, too. Then they carried on with what they were doing . . . cooking meals . . . cleaning the carpets . . . playing computer games.

The power that was making all the lights, cookers and computers work was electricity.

Electricity travels through wires. It flows along them in much the same way that water flows through pipes. The flow of electricity is called a current.

YEE HAA, LET'S GO, LADS!

Electric current is made in power stations and sent all over the country along a vast spiderweb of thick, heavy wires called power lines.

Electric current moves incredibly fast. It zips along at thousands of kilometres a second — quicker than you can blink!

Power stations turn one kind of energy (or power) into another. Most of the power the town used came from a hydro-electric (*high-drow-electric*) power station. It turned the energy of falling water into electricity.

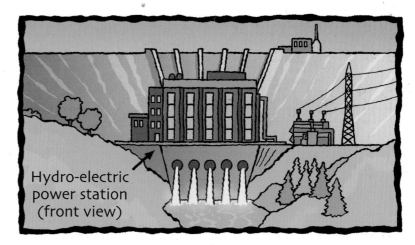

Hydro-electric power station (front view)

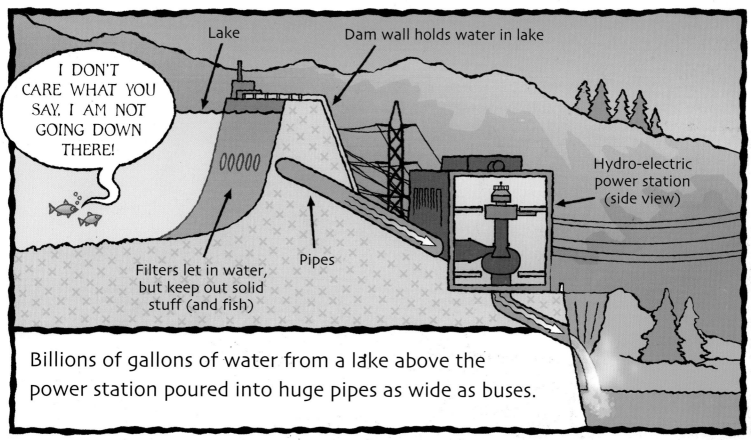

Lake

Dam wall holds water in lake

Hydro-electric power station (side view)

Filters let in water, but keep out solid stuff (and fish)

Pipes

Billions of gallons of water from a lake above the power station poured into huge pipes as wide as buses.

The pipes led to a row of machines inside the power station, called turbines. The turbines were like fat metal wheels, divided into sections by metal blades.

Turbine

Water in

Turbine

PHEW, THIS IS MAKING MY HEAD SPIN!

Metal blades

As the water rushed down each pipe, it crashed against the blades and made the turbine spin . . .

. . . just like a revolving door spins when people push through it.

Turbine

Water out

The water raced around the turbine and out the other side into a river, which tumbled away down the hillside.

The water's job was over. All it had to do was make the turbine spin, because . . .

SEE, I TOLD YOU IT WAS A WATERFALL MACHINE.

. . . as it spun, the turbine turned another wheel inside a machine called a generator.

The generator wheel was made of magnets, and magnets give out a special force called magnetism.

When the magnets whirled around, their magnetism made an electric current move inside some metal bands.

The current flashed from the metal bands into wires, which took it out of the power station . . .

Generator

LIFE'S ONE BIG WHIRL IN THIS PLACE.

Generator

Metal bands

Magnets

Turbine

. . . and into a transformer.

The transformer's job was to give the current a boost so that it could travel further along the power lines. Otherwise, it would gradually lose some of its strength and stop flowing.

Transformer

The current raced out of the transformer and into the power lines. These were lifted high above the ground on giant metal towers, called pylons. The pylons carried the lines away from the power station and across the countryside.

Meanwhile . . . high up in the sky the storm clouds billowed and tumbled.

Fat drops of rain splashed down, but the clouds weren't only stuffed with raindrops. They had millions of ice crystals in them, too.

Inside the tumbling clouds, the ice crystals bumped and jostled against each other. As they bounced about, they began to build up energy.

Before long, the clouds had so much energy they couldn't hold onto it any longer.

C R A A C K! A blinding flash of lightning leapt through the sky.

CRAACK

Lightning strikes in an instant and is hotter even than the surface of the Sun. It's made by another type of electricity called static electricity.

The lightning headed for the ground, but it didn't get there. Instead, it hit a power line.

The power line was carrying current towards the town. When the lightning hit it, everything came to a stop!

Lights went out. Televisions and radios died. Ovens stopped cooking and computer screens went blank.

It was as if someone had thrown a gigantic blanket over everything. It was a power failure!

Far away, at the control centre, an alarm flashed on a computer screen.

The alarm told the engineers there was a problem with one of the power lines, and they guessed the storm was to blame.

They knew they had to get electricity back to the people in that area as quickly as possible.

A team of engineers set off to inspect the line.

The engineers knew that the lightning strike must have sent a huge jolt of extra electricity into the power line. This extra jolt of electricity had set off the alarm, and safety switches at each end of the line had automatically turned the current off.

Before the current could be switched back on again, the engineers had to make sure that the line wasn't damaged.

Luckily, the line was okay. The switches were turned back on, and current whizzed along it again.

Everything was back to normal. The current flowed along the power lines until it reached the edge of the town. Then it was fed into another transformer. This transformer made the current weaker so it was safe for people to use.

The current that travels along the power lines is so powerful it would burn out most of the electrical machines we use.

Next, the current was split up and sent to different parts of the town. Some of it went into wires stretched between tall poles, and some of it went underground.

The poles carried the current away to a large factory on one side of the town . . .

. . . and to a large farm on the other side.

The current that went underground travelled along thick cables beneath roads and pavements.

Some of the cables led to street lights and traffic lights.

Others snaked off under paths, gates and gardens, into all of the offices, shops and houses in the town.

Inside the houses, each cable led to an electricity meter. This measured how much electricity the house used.

From the meter, another cable carried the current to a circuit-breaker. This works a bit like the safety switches on the power lines. If too much electricity suddenly floods into the house, it switches the current off.

From the circuit-breaker, wires spread out all over the place.

They travelled under floorboards,
inside walls and across ceilings.

They led to wall switches . . .
and lightbulbs . . . and plugs.

The plugs led to heaters and hairdryers . . .

. . . toasters and televisions . . .

. . . telephones,
fridges and washing
machines . . .

. . . and all of the things that we use every day because we have electricity!

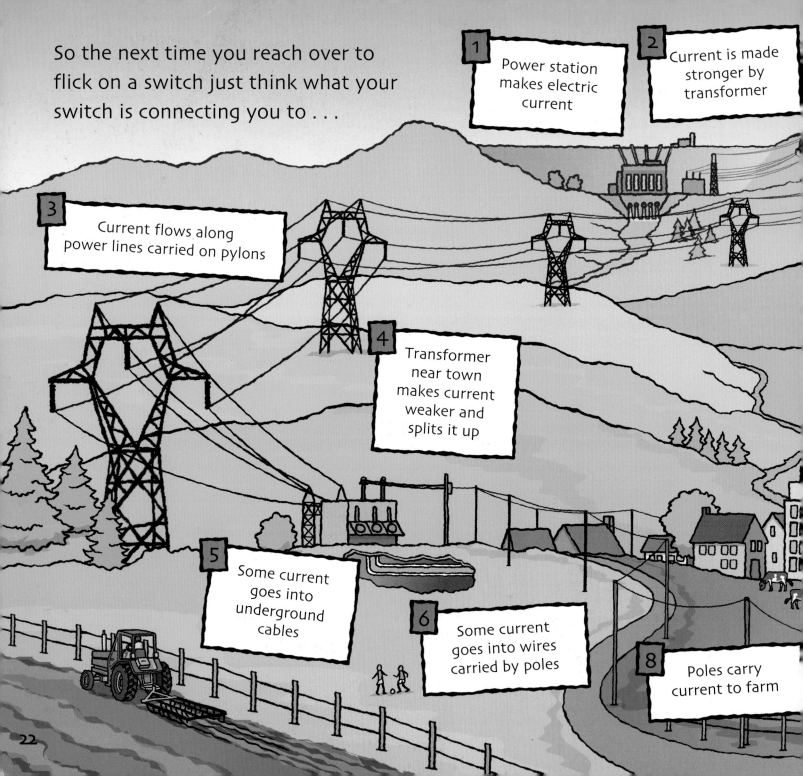

So the next time you reach over to flick on a switch just think what your switch is connecting you to . . .

1 Power station makes electric current

2 Current is made stronger by transformer

3 Current flows along power lines carried on pylons

4 Transformer near town makes current weaker and splits it up

5 Some current goes into underground cables

6 Some current goes into wires carried by poles

8 Poles carry current to farm

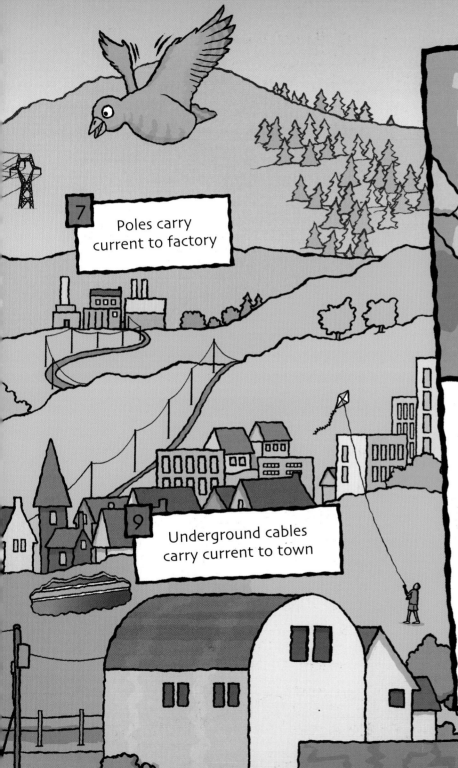

7 Poles carry current to factory

9 Underground cables carry current to town

. . . to thousands of metres of wires, and hundreds of pylons, machines and people. It's bringing electricity all the way from the power station to light your bedside lamp . . .

. . . all in the time that it takes to say, "Click"!

23

STEAMING ALONG

Hydro-electric power stations can only be built in places where lots of water from mountain lakes or rivers falls steeply downhill. Other power stations burn fuels, such as coal, oil or gas, to heat up water to make a high-pressure steam. Then the steam is used to turn the power station's turbines.

Fuel-burning power stations work well, but the smoke they make causes pollution and one day these fuels will run out. Scientists and engineers are looking for other ways of powering electricity turbines, such as using the energy from windmills.

BOXES OF ENERGY

I HOPE OUR BATTERY DOESN'T RUN OUT.

Not all electricity is carried along power lines. Some of it comes from batteries. Batteries have chemicals inside them that make small amounts of electricity. When the chemicals are used up, the battery stops working.

Batteries power all sorts of things from torches to toys and watches. They start the engine in a car and work its lights and heater. They are even used in submarines and spacecraft.

STATIC POWER

People make electric current travel along wires, but static electricity happens naturally all around us.

Static electricity makes your hair stand on end when you pull off a woolly hat. It also makes lightning. When too much static electricity builds up inside a cloud it looks for a way to escape. Lightning is electricity bursting out of the cloud!

Lightning often hits the highest thing within its reach. So the safest place to be when lightning is around is indoors!

WOW, THIS STATIC IS HAIR-RAISING STUFF.

WHAT A SHOCKER!

I FEEL SO STUNNING TODAY!

We aren't the only ones to make electricity. Some fish do it too! Electric fish have special muscles that work like generators. The fish use their electricity to shock enemies, or to stun or kill other animals for food.

The fish that gives the biggest shock is the electric eel. It lives in South American rivers and can grow as long as a ladder.

25

TRY IT AND SEE

LOOPING THE LOOP

Electric current has to flow around in a complete loop, called a circuit. If there is a gap or break in the circuit the current will stop flowing.

Current flows through some materials more easily than others. Things that carry current well are called 'conductors'. Things that don't are called 'insulators'.

Try this experiment to see how a circuit works and find out which materials make good conductors, and which don't.

You will need:
- A new 1.5 volt battery
- A 1.5 volt lightbulb and bulb holder
- Some single-core, plastic-coated wire
- Sticky tape, scissors, small screwdriver
- A collection of small objects
- An adult to give you a bit of help

1 Cut three lengths of wire about 20 cm long.

Next, carefully cut into the plastic coating about 15 mm from both ends of all three wires. Pull the plastic ends away, leaving a bit of bare wire.

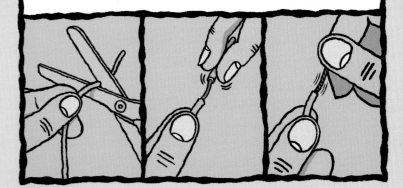

2 Take two pieces of wire and hook one end of each piece around the screws on the bulb holder. Screw them down firmly, then gently screw the bulb into the holder.

3 Tape the other end of one of the bulb wires to the bottom of the battery. Make sure the bare wire is touching the metal circle on the battery. Then take the third piece of wire and tape one end to the top of the battery.

4 You should now have all three pieces of wire connected to something, but still have two loose ends — **A** and **B**.

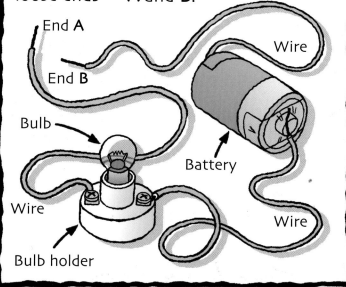

End **A**

End **B**

Wire

Bulb

Battery

Wire

Wire

Bulb holder

5 Touch ends **A** and **B** together. This completes the circuit and the bulb lights up. (If it doesn't, check your wires are firmly connected to the metal ends of the battery and the bulb holder.)

Try touching **A** and **B** to an object, such as a metal spoon. Both ends must touch the spoon. Does your bulb light up again? (Hint: metal is a good conductor.)

Now try some other objects, such as a plastic spoon, a pencil, an empty glass, a pencil rubber, a key, and a woollen glove. Which objects make the best conductors and which the best insulators?

ELECTRIFYING FACTS

Your body has millions of tiny electrical messages zipping around it all the time. The messages travel along your nerves from your eyes, ears, mouth, skin and muscles to your brain and back again. They even keep your heart beating.

A single stroke of lightning has enough energy in it to keep a lightbulb lit, day and night, for more than three months.

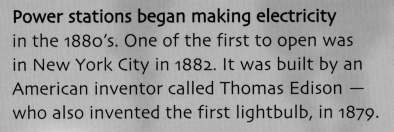

Power stations began making electricity in the 1880's. One of the first to open was in New York City in 1882. It was built by an American inventor called Thomas Edison — who also invented the first lightbulb, in 1879.

INDEX

SOME STUNNING WEBSITES TO VISIT

www.mos.org/sln/toe/toe.html = the "Theater of Electricity" website at the Museum of Science, Boston, USA. A brilliant site stuffed with information and activities to do with electricity.

www.energyquest.ca.gov = the website of the California Energy Commission, with games, projects and lots to links to other sites.

www.sciencemadesimple.com = a good general science site with projects, news and information on all sorts of different stuff.

For Louis
JB

For Phil and Alex
ML

First published in 2003 by
A & C Black Publishers Limited
37 Soho Square, London W1D 3QZ
www.acblack.com

Created for A & C Black Publishers Limited by
two's COMPANY
Copyright © Two's Company 2003

The rights of Jacqui Bailey and Matthew Lilly
to be identified as the author and the illustrator of this
work have been asserted by them in accordance with
the Copyrights, Designs and Patents Act 1988.

ISBN 0 7136 6257 3 (hbk)
ISBN 0 7136 6258 1 (pbk)

Printed in Hong Kong by Wing King Tong

A & C Black uses paper produced with elemental chlorine-free
pulp, harvested from managed sustainable forests.

With many thanks to Alan Smart at National Grid for his advice and help in the making of this book.